I Love Saturdays y domingos

by Alma Flor Ada

illustrated by Elivia Savadier

Aladdin Paperbacks

New York London Toronto Sydney

First Aladdin Paperbacks edition September 2004

Text copyright © 2002 by Alma Flor Ada
Illustrations copyright © 2002 by Elivia Savadier

ALADDIN PAPERBACKS
An imprint of Simon & Schuster
Children's Publishing Division
1230 Avenue of the Americas
New York, NY 10020

Also available in an Athenuem Books For Young Readers hardcover edition.
Designed by Abelardo Martinez
The text of this book was set in Caslon 224.
The illustrations are rendered in watercolor.

Manufactured in China
22 24 26 28 30 29 27 25 23

The Library of Congress has cataloged the hardcover edition as follows:
Ada, Alma Flor.
I love Saturdays y domingos / by Alma Flor Ada ;
illustrated by Elivia Savadier—1st ed.
p.   cm.
ISBN 978-0-689-31819-1 (hc.)
Summary: A young girl enjoys the similarities and the difference between
her English-speaking and Spanish-speaking grandparents.
[1. Grandparents—Fiction. 2. Mexican Americans—Fiction.]
PZ7.A1857 Iad 1998
[E]—dc20 94-003362
ISBN 978-0-689-87409-3 (pbk.)
0517 SCP

For Timothy Paul, Samantha Rose, Camila Rosa, Daniel
Antonio, Victoria Anne, Cristina Isabel, Jessica Emilia,
Nicholas Ryan, and their cousins Julian Paul, Emily Flor,
Ethan Franklin, Via, Aidan, and Robert Rey.
—A. F. A.

For Sadye with love from mama.
—E. S.

Saturdays and Sundays are my special days.

I call Sundays *domingos*, and you'll soon see why.

On Saturdays, I go visit Grandpa and Grandma.

Grandpa and Grandma are my father's parents.

They are always happy to see me.

I say, "Hi, Grandpa! Hi, Grandma!" as I walk in.

And they say, "Hello, sweetheart! How are you?

Hello, darling!"

I spend *los domingos* with *Abuelito y Abuelita.*
Abuelito y Abuelita are my mother's parents.
They are always happy to see me.

I say: —*¡Hola, Abuelito! ¡Hola, Abuelita!*— as I
get out of the car.

And they say: —*¡Hola, hijita! ¿Cómo estás?*
¡Hola, mi corazón!

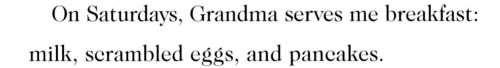

On Saturdays, Grandma serves me breakfast: milk, scrambled eggs, and pancakes.

The pancakes are spongy. I like to put a lot of honey on my pancakes.

Grandma asks me, "Do you like them sweetheart?"

And I answer, "Oh, yes, Grandma, I love them!"

Los domingos, Abuelita serves me a large glass of papaya juice and a plate of eggs called *huevos rancheros*. The *huevos rancheros* are wonderful. No one makes them better than *Abuelita*.

Abuelita asks me if I like them: —*¿Te gustan, hijita?*

First I need to swallow, and then I answer: —*Sí, Abuelita, ¡me encantan!*

Grandma has a tabby cat. Her name is Taffy.

I roll on the carpet and call, "Come, Taffy, let's play."

Abuelita has a dog. His name is *Canelo*. When I go out to the garden, *Canelo* follows me. I call out to him: —*Ven, Canelo. ¡Vamos a jugar!*

Grandma collects owls.

Every time that she and Grandpa go on a trip she brings back an owl for her collection.

Each one is different. I count them: One, two three, four, five, six, seven, eight, nine, ten, eleven, twelve . . . to see how her collection is growing.

Abuelita loves animals. When she was little she lived on a farm. She is glad that now they have a large backyard so she can keep chickens.

One of her hens has been sitting on her eggs for many days. Now the chicks have hatched. I count them: —*Uno, dos, tres, cuatro, cinco, seis, siete, ocho, nueve, diez, once, doce* . . .

One Saturday, Grandpa and Grandma play a movie about the circus for me on their VCR.

"I like the circus, especially the lions and tigers," says Grandpa.

"And the giraffes," says Grandma.

When Grandma and Grandpa ask me what part I like best, I answer:

"I like the mother elephant and her little elephant best."

Un domingo, Abuelito y Abuelita take me to a real circus.

—*Me encanta el circo, Abuelito*—I say.

—*Mira los leones y los tigres*—says *Abuelita*.

—*¡Y las jirafas!*—*Abuelito* adds.

When they ask me what I like best, I say:

—*La mamá elefanta y su elefantito.*

Grandpa has a beautiful aquarium. He keeps it very clean.

"Look at that big fish!" Grandpa says, and points to a big yellow fish.

"I like the little ones," I answer.

It's fun to watch the big and little fish. I watch, my nose pressed against the glass, for a long time.

Abuelito takes me to the seashore. He loves to walk by the ocean. We sit on the pier and look down at the water.

—*Mira el pez grande*— *Abuelito* says. He points to a big fish.

—*Me gustan los chiquitos*— I answer, and show him some little silver fish that are nibbling by a rock.

We stay at the pier *un buen rato,* for a long time.

Grandpa knows I love surprises.

One Saturday, when I arrive, he has blown up a bunch of balloons for me. The balloons look like a big bouquet of flowers: yellow, red, orange, blue, and green.

"What fun, Grandpa!" I say, and run with my balloons up and down the yard.

Un domingo, Abuelito also has a special surprise for me. He has made me a kite. The kite is made of colored paper and looks like a giant butterfly: *amarillo, rojo, anaranjado, azul, y verde.*

—*¡Qué divertido, Abuelito!*— I say. And I hold on to the string of my kite as it soars high in the air.

Grandpa likes to tell stories.

He tells me about how his mother, his father, and his older brother came to America in a big ship from Europe.

He also tells me about growing up in New York City. When he was a young boy, he delivered papers early in the morning, before school, to help his family.

Abuelito also likes to tell stories.

He tells me about the times when he was growing up on a *rancho* in Mexico. He worked in the fields when he was very young.

He also tells me how his father went to Texas, looking for work, and *Abuelito* was left in charge of his family. And he was only twelve!

Grandma loves to tell me about her grandmother whose parents came to California in a covered wagon. It was a long and difficult trip.

Grandma's grandmother was born on the trail. Later she became a teacher.

Grandma is very proud of her grandmother. I feel proud, too.

Abuelita loves to tell me about her *abuelita* and her *mamá.* Her *abuelita*'s family are Native Americans.

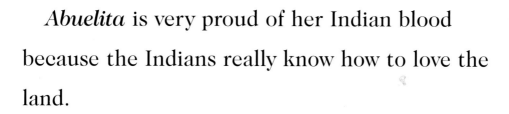

Abuelita is very proud of her Indian blood because the Indians really know how to love the land.

Abuelita feels *orgullo,* and I feel *orgullo,* too.

It's my birthday. This time, Grandpa and
Grandma come to our house. They have brought
me a new doll.

Grandma has made her a dress in my favorite
color.

"What a beautiful doll, Grandpa!" I tell him,
and I give him a big kiss.

"What a pretty blue dress! Thank you,
Grandma. I love you very much!" I say.

Abuelito y Abuelita also come.

Abuelito has made me a dollhouse.

Abuelita has made me a dress for my birthday party. The dress is exactly like my doll's dress. *Abuelita* and Grandma must have planned this surprise together!

—*¡Qué linda casa de muñecas, Abuelito! ¡Gracias!*— I say, and give *Abuelito* a big hug.

—*¡Y qué bonito vestido azul, Abuelita! El azul es mi color favorito*— I tell her. —*Gracias, Abuelita. Te quiero mucho.*

All my cousins and friends come to the party.
We gather together to break the *piñata* that my
Mom has filled with candy and gifts.

Abuelito is holding the rope to make the *piñata*
go up and down.

We all line up. The younger kids are in front.
Abuelita covers our eyes with a folded scarf so that
we can't see the *piñata*.

Finally I blow out the candles and cut the cake. Everyone sings "Happy birthday." Then, they sing *"Las mañanitas."* It goes like this:

Estas son las mañanitas
que cantaba el Rey David.
Hoy, por ser tu cumpleaños
te las cantamos a ti.

Despierta, mi amor, despierta

mira que ya amaneció

ya los pajaritos cantan

la luna ya se metió.

Some say, "Happy birthday!" and some say—
¡Feliz cumpleaños!

For me it's a wonderful day, *un día maravilloso.*

"*Las mañanitas*" is a traditional Mexican song. It is sung at birthdays. In some areas of Mexico, *mariachis* can be hired to serenade the person who is celebrating her or his birthday. The song says:

*This is the beautiful morning-song
which King David used to sing.
Today, because it is your birthday
we shall sing it for you.*

*Wake up, my loved one, wake up.
The sun has just come out.
The little birds are singing
and the moon has gone to sleep.*